My a Sound Box

by Jane Belk Moncure

illustrated by Pam Peltier

THE CHILD'S WORLD

ELGIN, ILLINOIS 60120

Library of Congress Cataloging in Publication Data

Moncure, Jane Belk.
  My "a" sound box.

  (Sound box books)
  Summary: When the contents of Little a's sound
box fall out, an astronaut helps him replace them
and takes him for an unexpected ride as well.
Features words beginning with the letter a.
  1. Children's stories, American. [1. Alphabet]
I. Peltier, Pam, ill. II. Title. III. Series.
PZ7.M739My 1984   [E]   84-17024
ISBN 0-89565-296-X

Distributed by Childrens Press, 1224 West Van Buren Street,
Chicago, Illinois 60607.

My "a" Sound Box

(This book concentrates on the short "a" sound in the story line. Words beginning with the long "a" sound are included at the end of the book.)

Little  had a box.

"I will find things that begin with my 'a' sound," he said.

"I will put them
into my sound  box."

Little a put on his hat and went
for a walk.

He found apples,
apples,
apples.

Did he put the apples into his box?

He did.

Little  found an alligator.

Did he put the alligator into the box
with the apples? He did.

Little found ants,
ants, ants.

Did he put the ants into the box
with the apples and the alligator?

He did.

Then Little  found arrows,
arrows,
arrows.

Guess where he put the arrows?

Next, Little  found an ax.

It was a toy ax.

Guess where he put the ax?

Now the box was so full...

the ants,

the arrows,

and the ax
fell out.

The apples
and the alligator

fell out too.

"Now who will help me
    fill my box?" said Little .

Just then an astronaut came by.

''I will help you,''  said the astronaut.

"We will fill your box."

Guess what happened next.

The astronaut took

Little  for a ride...

up, up, and away!

ants

alligator

arrows

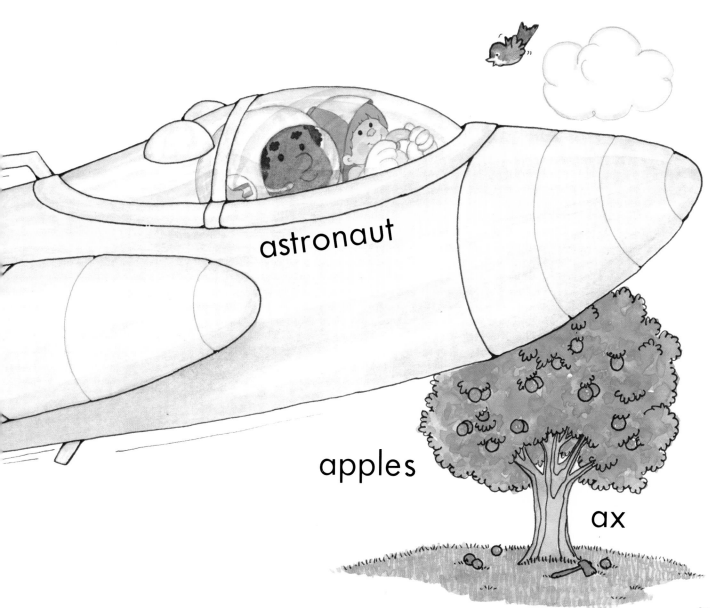

astronaut

apples

ax

Can you read these words with Little ?

antelope

acrobat

antlers

anchor

animals

ambulance

Little 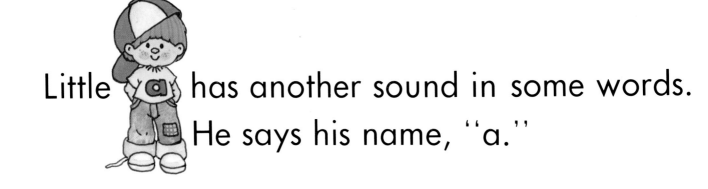 has another sound in some words.
He says his name, "a."

Can you read these words?
Listen for Little 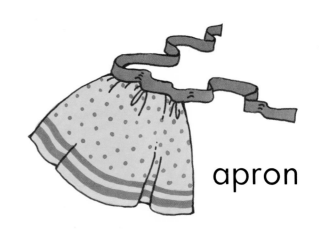's name.

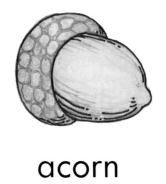

acorn

apron

APRIL

						1
2	3	4	5	6	7	8
9	10	11	12	13	14	15
16	17	18	19	20	21	22
23/30	24	25	26	27	28	29

angel

ape

About the Author

Jane Belk Moncure began her writing career when she was in kindergarten. She has never stopped writing. Many of her children's stories and poems have been published, to the delight of young readers, including her son Jim, whose childhood experiences found their way into many of her books.

Mrs. Moncure's writing is based upon an active career in early childhood education. A recipient of an M.A. degree from Columbia University, Mrs. Moncure has taught and directed nursery, kindergarten, and primary grade programs in California, New York, Virginia, and North Carolina. As a member of the faculties of Virginia Commonwealth University and the University of Richmond, she taught prospective teachers in early childhood education.

Mrs. Moncure has traveled extensively abroad, studying early childhood programs in the United Kingdom, The Netherlands, and Switzerland. She was the first president of the Virginia Association for Early Childhood Education and received its award for oustanding service to young children.

A resident of North Carolina, Mrs. Moncure is currently a full-time writer and educational consultant. She is married to Dr. James A. Moncure, former vice president of Elon College.